STORIES FROM THE WEST MIDLANDS

Edited By Tessa Mouat

Years of YoungWriters

First published in Great Britain in 2016 by:

Coltsfoot Drive
Peterborough
PE2 9BF
Telephone: 01733 890066
Website: www.youngwriters.co.uk

FOREWORD

Welcome to 'Spine-Chillers – Stories From The West Midlands'.

Inside this edition of spine-chilling 100-word tales from talented 11-18 year-old writers across the West Midlands, you'll find abandoned houses and asylums, mysterious beasts, demonic dolls and creepy Halloween nights that won't be forgotten. This is a collection of wonderfully spooky, shiver-inducing stories that investigate everything from the seemingly ordinary to the extraordinary. You'll meet a whole host of terrifying creatures and encounter unexplained sounds. You'll find out that no one can be trusted as flashlights reveal hidden horrors. It's great to see so many of you with unique styles of writing and positively terrifying tones of voice. They all gripped me from start to finish and ensured I checked under my desk for dark figures lurking below. I hope to see more of your creepy, fascinating tales in the future! One more thing – remember to leave the light on...

Tessa Mouat

CONTENTS

Lewis Thompson (13)	65	Malachi Clarke (13)	111
Hannah Archer (13)	66	Keon Liam Maxwell (13)	112
Charlie Vincent (12)	67	Adrian Findlay Owens (12)	113
Lucie Beddow	68	Jaiya Bhathal (12)	114
Mia Ward (11)	69	Sian Whittaker (12)	115
Owen Gregory (12)	70	Rafeeq De-Bessou (12)	116
Mia Bevan (12)	71	Kyle Swarnn (12)	117
Sean Mungure (13)	72	Theon Mukama (12)	118
Dillon Nayyer (13)	73	Faith Andrews (13)	119
Amber Boulton (12)	74	Jaiden J Hurlin (14)	120
Alex M J Jones (12)	75	Simran Gakhal (13)	121
Tia Louise Freeman (12)	76	Courtney Barker (13)	122
Zinal Patel (12)	77	James Elwell (12)	123
Luis Chrimes (12)	78	Jarvis Hartland (13)	124
Lauren Thomas (13)	79	Louise Walford (14)	125
Priya Madhar (12)	80	Louisa Childs (12)	126
Taliyah Sprackling (12)	81	Tyler Freeman (12)	127
Faith Warrender (11)	82	Tyler-Jade Linton-Phillips (13)	128
Symran Govindan (13)	83	Brandon Lee Baker (13)	129
Anna Lockley (13)	84	Jessica Thomas (12)	130
Lewis Chamberlain (13)	85	Darnell Boddie (13)	131
Udiet Kumar (12)	86	Inderpreet Rajasansi (13)	132
Vivek Toora (12)	87	Charley Michelle Love (13)	133
Ashton Ghera (12)	88	Georgina Williams (13)	134
Mia Bhatti (12)	89	Olivia Badial (11)	135
Ellis Savory (12)	90	Jagvir Singh (12)	136
Jessica Badial (11)	91	Caroline Barnes (12)	137
Mackaylah Sutton (12)	92	Vinnie-Lee Jordan (13)	138
Harry Smith (12)	93	Charlie Smith (12)	139
Alex Warner (12)	94	Kiitan Adeyeni (13)	140
Jamie Bromley (12)	95	Lily Kerry Benion (13)	141
Emily Boyle (12)	96	Shannon Hadlington (13)	142
Ajay Semic (13)	97	Dylan Clarke (13)	143
Alana Sophia Delgado (13)	98	Rhys Danks (12)	144
Dylan Thomas (13)	99	Mufaro Chuma (12)	145
Semhar Fesehaye (13)	100		

STOKE PARK SCHOOL, COVENTRY

Haylee Glover (13)	101
Calum Giles (12)	102
Daniel Lewis (13)	103
Courtney Marie Young (13)	104
Tarnjeet Singh (13)	105
Harvey Singh (12)	106
Angelicca Louise Ludwig (12)	107
Adam Watkins (13)	108
Ellie Hammond (13)	109
Victoria Marta Bury (12)	110

BobbiJay McBride (16)	146
Adrianna De-Blasio (14)	147
Zulfaqar Ali (14)	148
Yarna Patel (14)	149
Natalia Banas (13)	150
Augustine Uzochuckwu (14)	151
Sarah Robertson (17)	152

THE MINI SAGAS

Autumn Forest

His breath deepened as his legs lengthened, the sound of leaves crackled under his feet. Creepily, numbness from his toes slithered up his legs. Before he knew it, he was on the floor. Blackness.

He found himself under a plethora of autumn leaves. Above, he observed slender trees - he was in a forest. Drowning in thoughts, the weak man scrambled to his feet. Suddenly, he felt a cold hand grab his shoulder; it disappeared when he turned.

There was a strange presence lurking behind. He had to go. His legs tensed as he ran, looking for escape. Silence. Death.

Kirsty Squires (12)

Bristnall Hall Academy, Oldbury

GHOST

One word, five letters. Shocked by my long-lost friend. Her daunting, ghostly figure stirred me. She could beckon with a single slim finger. Then it happened. She drifted her deceased, deranged figure across my peripheral vision. Spread-eagled, she covered the only exit in the room. Moving her weightless body towards my own, she threw something.
The sharp beast's claw, filled with venom, punctured my neck. The blood oozed from my wound. Gulp. My body slowly broke. I waited to drown endlessly in a puddle of red. 'Spider!' she guffawed as I screamed.

RAJVIR SANDHU (12)
Bristnall Hall Academy, Oldbury

THE CREATURE THAT STOOD STILL

Running for my life, I didn't look behind at the gleaming in the shadows. I sprinted through the emerald-green forest, it seemed to be mocking me. There, standing in front of me, was a ghastly figure, so colossal that you couldn't miss it. I looked for somewhere else to turn. But I was cornered.
I felt fearful as it stormed towards me with a look its eye, as sharp as a razor. It headed towards me with an axe in its hand. My life flashed before my eyes. Then it raised the axe above my head. Death.

ALEEZA KHAN (13)

Bristnall Hall Academy, Oldbury

TALKING SPIRITS

'I really don't care!' I said as I slammed the door in my mum's face. I ran to the nearest forest. I felt like closing my eyes for a minute, so I did. Thoughts flowed past my mind, I felt sorry for the worm I stepped on.
'Open them,' I heard a voice say. I opened my eyes. What was I doing in a graveyard? Shadows followed me. I couldn't see anything. Whispers surrounded me. It was like the dead were calling my name. I tried hard to focus on my environment. Why was I walking slowly?
'Help me!'

MAHA FARA (13)
Bristnall Hall Academy, Oldbury

GRAVEYARD GRIEF

An ear-piercing scream. *This is abnormal,* thought Claire. Claire was normally approachable yet now she was alert, aggravated. Looking towards the graveyard, she saw a malicious man laugh mockingly at a young, vulnerable teenager. A feeling came over Claire like a tidal wave. Revulsion. Pure revulsion. Suddenly, the man's head turned like clockwork to face her. Eyes as black as coal. She pulled the curtains closed. *Ding!* The doorbell. Opening the door, Claire breathed deeply. It was the devilish man. He gave Claire a fortune cookie and walked away. It spoke, 'I'm coming!' She ignored it and bit down.

LINDA BURGESS (13)
Bristnall Hall Academy, Oldbury

Run

She went deep inside under the eerie presence of twilight. It was a spine-chilling, freezing night. Oblivious to the atmosphere around her, danger lurked, getting closer. Shadows wandered. Fallen leaves from a nearby tree danced around her feet. It felt as though something was coming, something sinister. The rustle of leaves came from behind. Slowly she moved from her stone-like position and turned to look. To her horror, she witnessed a woman on the ground, plastered in blood. Fear greeted her like an old friend. She leant down. The woman released one final word, 'Run.'

Chloe Hughes (12)
Bristnall Hall Academy, Oldbury

GIRL

The white-clothed girl sat on the wooden chair in the middle of the basement. There was a mysterious, peculiar feeling in the air. I took a step towards the hostile figure. The light started to flicker, I no longer felt safe. The light switched off, the girl began to scream. Petrified, I attempted to run up the stairs. Startled, the door slammed shut and threw me back down the stairs. I could no longer move, no matter how hard I tried to move my legs. Where had the girl gone? I heard her breathing...

BRAYDEN BIRCH (12)
Bristnall Hall Academy, Oldbury

THE VOICE

Trembling in fear, I approached the door. My hand shook and my heart pounded in my chest. The creak of the door echoed down the hallway. I heard a voice, 'Come here.' I slammed the door shut. There was silence for about two minutes. I slowly reached out for the door handle. I twisted the doorknob. My finger was twitching on the trigger as I opened the door. I saw a shadow down the hallway. I felt hands grab me from behind; I knew this was the end. No hope, just pain. I took my last breath.

ALEXANDER JAMES ONOFRIO-MILLS (13)
Bristnall Hall Academy, Oldbury

HALLWAYS

Speed; I knew I had to run as fast as I could. It was still behind me. The hallway was only a few metres wide but thousands of miles long. I ran through the door, the same one I'd gone through many times before. I was at the start again. I knew it would take a minute for it to get to the door. I looked at the paper in my pocket. It was a drawing. It hit me. I fell to the floor, the same words spinning around my head. Darkness, then white walls. 'It's time.'

CAMERON GROVE (12)
Bristnall Hall Academy, Oldbury

A Mask Of Remorse

I didn't mean to kill her - it was a flash!
A rolling mountainous storm overcame my eyes and caused
a great sky of anger to emerge from the depths of my brain.
So I just pushed her. She fell, only a pale face to remember.
I sit here in remorse wondering what I have done; I knew
the consequences would be severe.
A sharp pain eats away at me when I make any sudden
movements. Anxious, wounded, heartbroken - I stumble into
the cell and turn around and around.
I really didn't mean to kill her - I didn't!

JAMES GUESTS (15)
Lyng Hall School, Coventry

THE DAY OF DEATH

It was a day but not a standard day. It was a day of devastation and misery. As Marnie and her family went inside the church, they sniffled and sobbed, depressed. Everyone in the church took their seats and watched Lewis Keegan's body being carried peacefully. Some people bowed their heads in sorrow; others had eyes full of tears. After the ceremony the body was taken away.The vicar made his way home.

Suddenly, the doors banged, *slam!*

Figures appeared near devastated people.

'Argh! Ghosts!'

'We have come to curse you!'

Stab! That was the end of everyone and everything…

ANESAH AKHTAR (12)
Lyng Hall School, Coventry

UNTITLED

Boom! As I entered the church, the endless dark trees engulfed me.

Isolated in front of the abandoned church, the thunder signalled danger.

As I took a step further, the moonlight disappeared into the foggy, depressing clouds.

I walked slowly into the dirty, unbelievable church. Spiders and bats devoured it. I could smell danger coming closer and closer with every step I took. I was tiptoeing through the abandoned church. In the corner was a scary door. *Creak!* It opened. Before me stood a towering, oppressing figure. Then there was darkness...

GURSHARAN JANDU (12)
Lyng Hall School, Coventry

THE VISIONS OF OSCAR PHILLIPS

I run and run, a man is hunting me! I arise, realising that it was one of my annoying visions.

Bang! The door slams shut. An unknown person walks in, he begins to stare at me. He shockingly stands still like a statuesque figure. Sweating, I arise, acknowledging that it was just one of my maddening visions.

Slowly, he walks over and hands me a dagger. I'm frustrated so I take the dagger. Shivering and shaking, I close my eyes.

'We are here to today to commemorate the death of Oscar Phillips,' says the priest.

MIA LINDSAY (12)
Lyng Hall School, Coventry

THE SHADOW UNDER MY BED

It was thundering that night, the television turned off as a gust of wind smashed into the window. Shivers shot up my spine.
Suddenly, my mum called me upstairs and said, 'It's time for bed.'
On my way up the creaky stairs I thought I heard someone whisper my name, I ignored it because I thought it was just in my mind.
I got myself into bed and as I started to fall asleep I felt vibrations under my bed. I slowly looked to see what was there. As I saw it, a feeling of torment overcame me.

ISABELLA KAMFER (12)
Lyng Hall School, Coventry

THE BABYSITTING JOB

Rain was pouring over Cameron's head as he sprinted towards the gigantic, dark house. Trees towered over, giving him an intimidating glare.

Cameron unlocked the door to the house. He gingerly walked towards his cousin's room and opened the door. He was engulfed by shadows and met with eyes.

They weren't Jacob's eyes but a doll's!

Cameron sprinted towards the forest. He quickly ran out of breath, he looked down and came face-to-face with the blood-covered doll.

EMILY DANIELS (12)
Lyng Hall School, Coventry

INSANE

She anxiously stared at another envelope, wishing to know what was inside. Her finger slid across the page. 'You did it! You're guilty, guilty, guilty!'
The little girl screamed, crying, throwing herself from wall to wall. *Slam!*
A whisper grew louder in the distance. She stood on her battered feet, struggling to walk. She followed her gaze to the most mesmerising glow. Not knowing what to do, she leapt for the soul. A hand stopped her. Drowning in her own fear, her piercing eyes stared at the flickering light. Darkness appeared, it consumed her.

ABIGAIL TURNBALL (12)

Lyng Hall School, Coventry

DEADLY AFRAID

My stomach painfully churned as the taste of scarlet blood crawled back up my throat. It caused me to retch in disbelief. Was I going to die tonight?

Petrified, the skin from my bony fingers slit open, leaving patches of flesh spilling out. Pain spread through my body like an agonising disease. Was this death?

Six feet under, my lifeless corpse lay, infested with flies and spiders. They crept over me, leaving marks of possession. They enclosed me, trying to squirm my way out was useless. Isolated, the compact space suffocated me. What was happening? A shattered soul.

KASHMALA KHAN (12)

Lyng Hall School, Coventry

THE SPIRIT OF THE WOODS

After a season of real darkness, my heart sank into a pit of gloom. Terrified, concerned and scared, I ran through the depressing woods. Out of nowhere a loud crash alarmed me, causing me to jump. The sound echoed throughout my mind. No matter how much I tried, it wouldn't stop.
A few moments later, I realised it was just a couple of fireworks. Even though I knew the truth, the slightest sound made my heart skip a beat. A sudden gust of wind brushed over my face. I felt someone watching my back. Was someone there?
'Argh!'

KANAGAH SARVANANTHALINGAM (12)
Lyng Hall School, Coventry

THE BLOODY NIGHT

It was 11:50pm, a piercing scream rang through my ears. I got up quietly, anxious and frightened, I took fearful steps down the hallway. Trails of blood led from my parents' bedroom.

Suddenly, spine-chilling thoughts crept into my head. Where had they gone? Why had they gone? I nearly collapsed at the thought of my beloved parents being dead.

Grabbing my shoes and jacket, I stumbled out of the house, searching for my loved ones. My heart sank; hope vanished into the fear that flooded my body. I was lost.

ARIENE HOYTE-SUTHERLAND (12)
Lyng Hall School, Coventry

3... 2... 1... Gone!

Furious, the clouds thundered and roared. With one striking blow, the lightning cut through the tree. The three girls kept treading, grieving their mother's death. How she ended up in the grave was a painful mystery. A crimson rose was held in each of their pale hands.

Suddenly, a deafening screech bellowed from behind. A single distraction made the children look. Only two girls were left ambling. As they tried to run to safety, an immense gulp of wind captured another child. Frightened, disturbed and agitated, the last fragile girl froze as the black shadow sank her soul.

Komal Chauhan (12)

Lyng Hall School, Coventry

LET'S GO CAMPING!

I've never felt so alive before. The sun was glimmering on Jack and I, sitting in the sapphire sky. Later on, we went to find wood. Once we got back I made my tent. I collapsed with exhaustion.

3am: Suddenly, I woke up. *Bang!* I heard noises! I quickly rushed over to my phone to text Jack, but there was no reception! The noise was getting closer and closer. My chest got tighter and tighter. It seemed like there was a spiked collar around my neck. I slowly stared at the tent door. A shaded figure arose...

KAMERON LALLI (12)
Lyng Hall School, Coventry

THE CHAMBER OF HORROR

There it was - it stood like a predator about to attack its prey, about to eat its innocent flesh in the abandoned forest. Nobody dared to come in. Lightning struck and thunder roared. I stepped closer and closer, knowing that whoever went in would be tortured and murdered. I had to find out the truth. What was lurking behind that crooked, cobwebbed door? Blood dripped from the windows as the faces of little children struck my soul, asking me to join them. Graves moaned at me as a vague figure appeared!
'The chamber of horror has been reopened.'

KARINA SANDHU (12)

Lyng Hall School, Coventry

THE FOREST

It was 9:30pm, John and I went into the forest to explore.
My parents didn't even know I'd gone outside.
Hopefully they wouldn't notice.
As I approached a tree, a branch snapped and it almost
landed on me. It looked like it had snapped with some force.
I looked around to see if John was behind. He wasn't. The
clouds began to separate, the moon was bright. Wolves
were howling, owls were hooting. Suddenly, a mysterious
figure tapped my shoulder. I thought it was John. When I
turned around nobody was there.

MELVIN MALISSA (12)
Lyng Hall School, Coventry

Untitled

One night, Angie invited her friends over to her house. They were telling horror stories about Bloody Mary. 'She was a girl, killed by her husband and her soul entered all the mirrors in the world.' Angie didn't believe it. She said, 'Bloody Mary,' three times into the mirror.

Suddenly, her reflection twisted, then they heard someone knocking at the door. It was her dad. When no one answered he knocked the door down. The spirit tried to enter Angie but she broke the mirror! The demon disappeared. Or had it?

Roberta Simidreanu (12)

Lyng Hall School, Coventry

THE HUMAN HOUSE

My confused mind watched the smoky mist suffocate the abandoned house. Black crows flew around the chimney, attracted to whatever was inside. Shaking, the tall, dark trees stood behind the house, not wanting to come out. Who knows who lived here? No wonder no one walked down that street. Shivering, the house looked at me, its windows cracked, its walls crumbled, its roof weakened and its door open. The house whispered to me, 'Come, come in.' The spine-chilling voice crept towards me. Distracted, the smell of cookies filled my nose. A hand grabbed me, taking me inside...

SANDEEP KAUR BALREY (12)
Lyng Hall School, Coventry

TRESPASSERS

Knock, knock! I banged on the door. *Knock, knock!* Silly humans came to this place on purpose. *Knock, knock!* Their terrified screams filled me with delight. I decided to drift through the quiet door. Although I was just a shadow, I was capable of anything. I could hear their hearts pounding in their chests. It looked like they were paralysed in fear. It wouldn't be hard to kill them. They shouldn't have risked their lives to experience paranormal activity. I had an advantage, I was like a wolf in a sheep pen. I was going to get rid of them.

ALEXIS JEAVONS (12)
Lyng Hall School, Coventry

HALLUCINATIONS

Anxious and nervous, bored and lonely, I was in the hospital, clutching on to dear life. I squeezed Freddy, my plush toy, as I laid on my deathbed. Lights flickered as something scratched me. I looked down to see Freddy peering into my soul with his white beady eyes. He scratched me with his unrealistically sharp claws. A giant grin appeared on his face, revealing a pair of blade-like teeth. There were no sounds other than my heartbeat thudding in my chest continuously. I felt Freddy breathing on my neck. The final words I heard were, 'See you in Hell.'

SAMEER KHAN (12)
Lyng Hall School, Coventry

UNTITLED

One stormy night, Max was driving a car down the highway. Suddenly, he saw a path leading to a walnut house. Intrigued, Max exited the car and walked down the windy path. The trees formed a canopy above him. He approached the dark, miserable house and found the entrance. Suddenly, there was a screeching noise! Max thought it was snakes or bats. He started to investigate. He found a room. It was dark and the curtains were shut. He entered and felt a breeze. Then he felt something fly past his shoulder. Crimson began to drip from his ear...

MAKSIMS FOMINS (12)

Lyng Hall School, Coventry

THE CREATURE

Tap! Tap! Tap! Arousing from my slumber, blood ran down my fragile skin. *Crash!* Bolting to the spacious bathroom, the bath's brim was overflowing with crimson blood. Broken bones drifted on the top. Drenched, stained towels were flung on the floor. *Crash!* Scrambling, I raced along the spiralled narrow stairs and headed towards the kitchen. Bulging, my eyes glimpsed the kitchen knife disguised by blood. Dashing upstairs, I wanted to hide from the danger. As I crept under my bed, the whole world plummeted into darkness...

SHEERAH BASSI (12)
Lyng Hall School, Coventry

LITTLE DEAD RIDING HOOD

'Argh!' I screamed as someone ran past me, almost cutting me in half. Dropping to the floor, a bolt of lightning struck about a metre away. I was dead, then a second bolt of lightning struck, hitting me. Rising from the dead, I spotted the not so big bad wolf. I thought he looked tasty so I followed him to a little wooden cabin. I snuck in quietly and spotted an even bigger, tastier wolf so I ate them both. 'Yum!' You may think you're safe behind the pages of this book, but you're next! Readers, beware!

SUMMER WHITTLE (11)
Lyng Hall School, Coventry

HALLUCINATIONS

The pills! Surely it must be the pills that are causing these visions, the shadows, the noises. They are driving me insane! I tell myself that I'm alone but I don't believe it. The shadows creep across the wall, slowing to look at me. I called the doctor earlier today, to make sure that the pills were still in my system. Sounds of banging and crashing come from the kitchen downstairs. That's when the phone rings, making me jump out my skin. The doctor's voice comes from the other side of the phone, 'The pills aren't in your system.'

MASON KIERNAN (12)
Lyng Hall School, Coventry

GOOD MORNING

6am: I open my eyes, my vision still blurry. The sound of my alarm is all I can hear. I go to turn off the roaring sound, only to realise every muscle in my body has frozen. I must be dreaming. I try again. This time I realise it's no dream but horrifying reality. My room's pitch-black, the light on my alarm has disappeared. As I think it can't get any worse, through the darkness I feel the touch of long, skinny, freezing cold fingers running up my toes. I scream, cry and shake, nothing releases me from the spell.

SENDIJA ABELE (12)
Lyng Hall School, Coventry

HAUNTED HOUSE

It was a dark, cold night, a little boy, James, wandered through the deep, silent forest. He looked to the left to see leaves falling from the old jagged branches. To the right of him he could see insects munching on leaves and huge creatures that looked like bears lurking nearby. With no hesitation, James ran faster than the blink of an eye. He ran, frightened, down the vast forest towards the haunted house. Staring at his death, he could see holes in the walls. He could see smashed windows. He entered the house and met his horrifying death.

OLIVER WOAN (12)
Lyng Hall School, Coventry

The Bus Ride

10pm: Alone on the bus, deadly silence fills the air. The horrifying eyes of the driver glare into mine like a hypnotist penetrating my innocent mind. We stop. The driver slowly begins to edge towards me, a meat cleaver in one hand, a bloody chainsaw in the other. Paralysed, I sit and stare. My blood turns cold. Unable to move, I stay stuck, awaiting my unfortunate fate. His smirk continues to grow on his partially worn face. The bus starts to move towards a dark tunnel. A faint whisper is heard in the distance as we come to a halt...

KIYA BENNETT (12)
Lyng Hall School, Coventry

THE HOUSE WITH NO RETREAT

I slowly approached the gate of the horrifying house. Hell's gates. Terrified, a shiver went down my spine. I was curious, I wondered what lay inside. Running towards the house of hell itself, I went through the ginormous gates. I fell down a giant hole. I rapidly searched the area where I'd fallen, there was an airbed. It had broken my fall but was now punctured, there was a tiny little window in the corner of the room. Questions raced through my mind. Suddenly, there was a huge bang...

JOSHUA SHANNON (12)
Lyng Hall School, Coventry

THE HOTEL

The hotel stares down at them like a beast stalking its prey. They can't turn back now. The two boys walk through the doors, there is no power. Ghastly noises fill the silent night. One boy hears an ear-bursting scream. He turns around to find James hanging from the ceiling. This funny dare has turned into a race for survival. He tries to run to the doors but they slam shut. He runs up the nearest staircase. There is a window! He runs towards it but something falls. He looks up and the devil is hanging from the light.

HARRY WILSON (12)

Lyng Hall School, Coventry

THE ECHOING FROM THE WELL

Step... Crunch... Step... Splat! The sound of the echoing well screeches and snaps. As I walk towards it, it gets quieter. I am left with the silence of death and horror. Day and night I wake up to the sound of screaming. I hide under my sheets. I switch on the torch light, hoping that the soul taker hasn't come to leave me breathless. I slowly creep out of my room, leading myself to the garden. Where am I going? What am I thinking? *Bang!* The well opens, I freeze and there it is...

HAZEL MARUMO (12)
Lyng Hall School, Coventry

THE LIVING GHOST

At that moment the truth dawned on me. Joseph was dead. As I walked through a dark alleyway, a chill shot through my neck. Suddenly everything went black. A pain in my spine made me shoot up. My vision was a blur but I could make out a white, hazy figure. My claret heart cascaded into a million pieces. Dark crimson blood dripped from his disfigured face. It was him! He advanced forward. I slipped in a pool of scarlet blood. Was he hurt? Wait - it was my blood! I screamed in terror, but nothing came out.

SHABBA BASSI (12)
Lyng Hall School, Coventry

THE CRASH

Driving in my car after a long day of work, my eyes are slowly shutting down and my energy levels are slowly decreasing. I start imagining things that aren't there, thinking I will bump into them. I end up turning my car the wrong way. *Boom!* I crash into a car. I can hear the police coming, the man in the car is taken to the hospital. Somehow I'm alright. The police are still here, I hear another crash, more and more people dead. One crash, another crash - here comes another one.

BRIGITTE BERKOH (12)
Lyng Hall School, Coventry

THE GRAVEYARD

I stared at the graveyard, my friends had dared me to go in but none of them came. Its rusty handle creaked as I opened it. Desolate. No living soul had stepped foot in here. Then I walked closer to the church that stood at the back. Before I could take another step, something made me stop. Beams of sweat ran down my face. A shiver ran down my spine. There was a creak coming from behind me. The gate was closed. I didn't close it. Eerie silence screamed in my ears. A cold hand touched my back...

SHARESE JOHNSTON
Lyng Hall School, Coventry

WHERE'S THE EASTER BUNNY?

'Max, it's your big day!'

'Coming!' Max bolted down the staircase.

'Happy birthday, Max!'

'Thanks Grandma.'

'Since your birthday is the same date as Easter this year, I've got a box of chocolates upstairs for you!'

'Is the Easter bunny coming then?'

'No.'

Max looked bewildered.

'Oh my dearest dear, a much darker spirit will be coming this year.'

'Can I go to the cinema with my friends?'

'Of course you can.'

Max decided to depart the house as darkness fell. Was that a wise decision? When he arrived at the cinema, no one was there.

'Shh, we're here.'

SAMUEL ADETOGUN (11)
Moseley Park School, Bilston

ONE HALLOWEEN NIGHT!

'Boo!'

'Why did you scare me like that, Jake?' Michael yelled. Jake explained that ghosts didn't exist. Michael begged to differ. 'I will prove to you that paranormal activity doesn't exist,' vowed Jake.

Once Michael and Jake arrived at the Halloween haunted house, Jake took out his ghost-busting equipment to detect if ghosts existed. Michael trembled as he felt gusts of wind. He heard the wallpaper slowly peeling.

'There's nothing to be afraid of,' Jake said. Suddenly his equipment began buffering! *Tap, tap, tap.* Jake felt it. *Poof!* Jake disappeared. What would Michael do?

CHIKOMBORERO BAKE MADANHI (12)

Moseley Park School, Bilston

YOU HAVE REACHED THE DEATH ZONE!

'You have now reached the Death Zone.'
When we heard this we started to get worried because we didn't know who had said it. Chanell and I thought it would be alright until the woman grabbed us and ripped our teeth out. Blood squirted everywhere, then she ripped out our eyes. The woman then cut our bodies up and made us into dolls. She put us outside the graveyard.
One day, a boy named Jordan was walking past. 'Come along, boo! Watch what we give to you!'
People now know not to go down to the graveyard at night.

SIAN READ (13)
Moseley Park School, Bilston

Untitled

Suddenly, Dylan, Keon and Matthew rushed through my front door like it wasn't there. When they got upstairs I asked them if they wanted to come through to the forest with me.

As we were walking through the forest we stumbled across an old abandoned school. Keon, Matthew, Dylan and I went in. As we entered the corridor, we saw three black shadows. As they turned around, we saw they had a knife, an axe and a sledgehammer! They tilted their heads and came towards us, wherever we ran they were there...

Alex Arrowsmith (11)

Moseley Park School, Bilston

ANONYMOUS

The weather outside was dull. George was instantly ordered to get straight to work. He went to his computer but noticed that something wasn't right. Something was missing. He checked his computer to see if everything was fine. It wasn't. The screen saver was the faces of a notorious group who had killed a large number of people. 'I thought I got rid of them?' Out of nowhere the speakers turned on. 'Expect us!' Everything around him turned off.

'It was almost time for my break anyway.' Then bangs and blinding flashes came with screams. What was going on?

NATHANIEL GARTH ROSE-GREEN (12)

Moseley Park School, Bilston

SAW

It started as a dare. Slowly, we strolled up to the building that towered over us. Suddenly, the door creaked open. We wandered around for a few minutes. A dark figure appeared. 'Stevie? What's that?'
Stevie glared at me. 'I don't know.'
The figure turned around and sprinted towards us. 'Run!' I bellowed. I could hear his footsteps behind me. I could smell the horrible stench of decaying bodies. As we ran, the rooms got darker and darker until it was pitch-black. There was the door. I sprinted as fast as I could. He was gone. We got out.

BILLY EVANS (12)
Moseley Park School, Bilston

THE TRINITY

'Looks like it's empty,' Josie said. Silence. She looked around. *Rumble!* The next thing she knew she was on the floor, cold and disorientated. The place she was in was haunted by The Trinity. They were sisters that killed each other and were now phantoms.

Josie ran into a room to find food and heat. *Click!* The door locked. A phantom hovered above her with a knife in hand. 'You have entered our lair! Now you must join us!' She backed away and looked closer.

She saw someone else. 'Mother?'

ABENA ADU-BOATENG (12)
Moseley Park School, Bilston

Never Sleep Again

I had trouble sleeping. I focused my eyes on two streetlights that flickered every few seconds, I soon fell asleep.

The next night the exact same sleeping troubles came back and I focused my eyes on the same streetlights. 'That's strange. They seem to have moved,' I said quietly. As soon as I said that, they went out.

The following morning, I looked outside to see if anyone was fixing the dead lights. To my dismay there weren't even any lights there. Only claw marks. Something had been perched there, watching me...

Angela Jean Buerke (12)
Moseley Park School, Bilston

THE FOREST

One night, there was a boy in the forest. That same night a lost man was walking his dog. The man shouted, 'Somebody help me!'

The boy heard and ran towards the voice. The boy asked, 'Why did you shout?' The boy looked around and scanned the area. There was nothing there. The boy saw the man run through the forest and into a small white car.

The next week, in the same forest, he saw the man's dog with a newspaper next to it. It read: 'Man killed by strange man'. Then the boy went into a deep sleep.

KIA WALKER (12)
Moseley Park School, Bilston

THE SOLDIER OF DEATH

On a stormy night, a family moved to a new house, they didn't know what they were about to experience. The walls were red and black with stripes.

On the first night, a young boy woke up. He heard a scream from a woman and noticed blood on the walls.

The next day, the boy's mum saw a dark figure. *Smash!* A plate was pushed by an unnatural force. All she saw then were burning red eyes. The mother went to a paranormal expert and found out the house was haunted by a murderous soldier. They were never seen again.

SHANE MURPHY (13)

Moseley Park School, Bilston

DER EISENDRACHE

Takeo and Dempsey were talking about who they had killed in war. They mentioned who they had killed last. 'Edward Richtofen.'

Later that night, they found themselves in a castle called 'Der Eisendrache'. They knew it was a German word that translated to 'the iron dragon'. They immediately got scared when they saw dragon statues. They walked down some stairs and immediately stopped, horrified. They heard a bellowing roar. After that, they saw four paintings, Takeo knew the story the paintings were telling. Before he could explain, a familiar voice whispered, 'Remember me? Edward Richtofen!'

KRISTIAN RATHBONE
Moseley Park School, Bilston

Join Us!

Darkness surrounded us. The only source of light was the moon projecting through the thick canopy of trees.
Footprints disturbed the perfect carpet of snow until our path came to an abrupt stop. A tall building loomed over us, 'We're here!' I exclaimed. After exploring the eerie building we couldn't find Isaac. That was until a loud banging sound began echoing from down the hall. Thinking it was him, we flung the door open, revealing Isaac rocking back and forth. 'Isaac!' we yelled.
Slowly turning around, showing his black eyes, he whispered, 'Join us!' as people began to gather.

Caitlin Riley (13)
Moseley Park School, Bilston

THE REMAINING FOUR

Five were taken. Four came back. 'Aria, Spencer, Jasmine and Silver!' Their mother's face brightened. Then it dropped. 'Hermione?' she questioned. Not back yet. Whilst they were with the devilish monstrosity, their father had passed away. Sadly, their holder never set them be free for the funeral. At the graveyard the sisters were hand in hand, scurrying across the chilling stone ground. They all separated in search of the grave, until Jasmine made a discovery. Hermione was there! She took a gasp of air. 'Who's next?' she cackled. her eyes glistened horrifically in the dark.

JASPRIYA BHAMRA (12)
Moseley Park School, Bilston

DEAD BY DAYLIGHT

'Let's camp here for the night,' I whispered to myself. I was suspicious… It was a farm with tall crops looming above. A derelict shed seemed to have someone in there… and a blood-gored slaughterhouse, where the soulless eyes of the cows seemed to glare at me… But my curiosity got the better of me, I decided to explore, but as I stood up I heard a blood-curdling screech 'Argh!' I leapt into the crops… I could feel my heart pounding… I heard church bells ringing. I heard someone laugh maniacally.
'Please… argh!'

BRENDON JAMAIN WASARIREVU (12)
Moseley Park School, Bilston

DEATH DAY

On a sunny day, some friends met at The Flames. Little did they know, there were supernatural creatures living there. After dusk they explored the abandoned house. Together, Hermione, Nevaeh and Charlie entered the house. Ty was supposed to be there but he wasn't. The full moon rose, wails were heard and a werewolf appeared from nowhere. Then a man, Damian, came, grabbed a silver fork and ran like lightning. He stabbed the wolf. Damian screamed, 'Run, before I kill you!' His eyes were red, his veins popped. He ripped everyone apart, there was blood everywhere.

CHLOE GAVIN (12)
Moseley Park School, Bilston

The Hospital

The temperature instantly dropped as cold as ice. I couldn't see anything but a dusty, creepy hallway. I turned to my friends and said, 'It's alright, come in!'
As soon as I said it, *bang!* The door slammed shut behind me. I tried to pull it but it wouldn't budge. I called for my friends but there no response. Suddenly, I heard a distant sound. 'Hello?' I said bravely. I heard steps getting louder and louder. I could see a dark figure limping down the hall. One blink and it vanished! Trembling, I tugged the door. A cold hand grabbed me...

Alicia Wilson (12)
Moseley Park School, Bilston

HORRIBLE CATHERINE

'Ha, huh!' panted Catherine, she'd been running for days. She found herself at an old abandoned castle. She hopped and leapt over to the castle. As soon as she got there she could see cobwebs and taste dampness. She stayed and as the nights passed it got stranger and stranger until one night glass was broken. Catherine ran downstairs and all over the wall was 'Nathaniel' in red paint. Then suddenly two ghosts appeared, one was called Nathaniel and the other Phil. They spun around her and locked her in a cupboard. Months later, she escaped as a monster.

LEESHA SHANIA HARVEY (12)

Moseley Park School, Bilston

INSIDE

When she moved to the monastery of peace, she thought she had escaped all the evil in the world. But people began to disappear. One night, the nun felt a sharp pain in her chest and the religious cross turned upside down. Suddenly, the doors swung open. The leaves flew into the building. 'What's happening?' she said to herself. She ran as fast as lightning to the graveyard. The sky was full of spirits and smoky grey clouds. She broke down crying as she asked herself, 'Why am I the last one?'
'It's because the demon is inside you!'

JESSICA JONES (13)
Moseley Park School, Bilston

THE TOXIC SPOTS

'Stop popping your spots!' Mum screamed. 'You'll make it worse!' But the spots, which had grown bigger and bigger were so annoying. The spots lay on the boy's skin, embedded like splinters. 'It'll poison you if you don't stop!' his mum continued.

When she'd fallen asleep the young boy searched and scanned for something to pop his spots with. The young boy gave up and hopped into bed and tried his best to not scratch and pop them. Night by night, the toxic spots grew more toxic and the young boy eventually died.

JACK JONES (12)
Moseley Park School, Bilston

Spooky Night

On Halloween night, Harry went out trick or treating. He came across an abandoned house and thought to himself, *if I go in there I'll be the bravest person ever*. So he walked slowly up to the door and opened it. The door slammed behind him. *Bang*. He started to walk around and suddenly he heard screaming upstairs. He stood there in horror.
He then heard footsteps and a voice saying, 'I'm after you!' He ran to the door but the door wouldn't open. He was stuck in the house with this loud, mysterious thing. Would he get out?

Zoe Stackhouse (13)

Moseley Park School, Bilston

THE CROW

Across the field, the dark, black, beady eyes stared at me. Each second was another moment of torture and horror. Its sophisticated glare sent a shiver down my spinal cord, making me shake tremendously. It viciously squawked and flew away, leaving me stunned and surprised. I was about to leave, when I felt a cold breath travel down my back. I turned sharply on my heel and found nothing. I looked back to check I was alone. I was. It was silent. Out of nowhere I heard a soft whisper calling my name. 'Ellie!' Then again, 'Ellie!'
'Argh!'

LASHAE MUNROE-DINHAM (13)
Moseley Park School, Bilston

THE LIGHTNING

As I watched the darkness quickly sweep over the gloomy, grey graveyard, I suddenly realised I was running out of time. I had to cut through the graveyard if I ever wanted to get home before midnight.

Within just a few steps into the graveyard my shoes were already drenched in soggy, black mud. I continued walking, gaining speed with every step. Lightning flashed, shivers crept down my spine. Lightning flashed again and revealed a hand rising from its grave. And with a final flash of lighting the hand slowly started moving. It was coming for *me*.

RENAE SOYINKA (13)
Moseley Park School, Bilston

THE ABANDONED THEME PARK

One stormy night, two boys, who were best of friends, stumbled across an old, abandoned theme park. John and Luke decided to break into the theme park. Luke was drawn to the carousel. There was something strange lurking around but Luke didn't notice. He pretended to be a cowboy. Suddenly, the carousel started to spin. It started slowly, then got quicker and quicker. Suddenly, it spun out of control. Luke flew off the carousel, over the top of the headless horse. John ran and as he looked back everything was gone.

'Where's Luke?'

COURTNEY SKITT (11)
Moseley Park School, Bilston

ECHO OF THE PAST

I took a deep breath as I slowly shuffled towards the abandoned villa. I readied my special night vision camera. I was going to need it. From what I heard most people didn't come back. I bet it was just a bunch of foolish myths. As I walked through the villa I could have sworn I heard noises. Then I heard the terrorising howl of a wolf mixed with something, something reptilian. I charged through the hallways, remembering what I'd done before now. The experiments! The accident! The clicking defect! *Click! Click!* 'Oh no!'

CHARLOTTE OWEN (12)

Moseley Park School, Bilston

THE PATH

As she hurried down the damp canal path, a shady man approached her. Trying to walk faster, the woman's heel broke and she fell down with a thud. The silhouette of the man grabbed the woman's arm. Her heart raced. The mysterious man was holding a gun and he said, 'You dropped this.'

Weak at the legs, the woman's eyes filled with tears as she thought that it was the end. The man asked if the revolver was hers. He sounded demanding. The woman kept quiet. The man moved the gun towards the woman's head. *Click! Bang!*

LEWIS THOMPSON (13)

Moseley Park School, Bilston

Hide-'n'-Seek...

'Our game of hide-'n'-seek has just begun.'
Realising that I knew her, I screamed out her name, she looked at me and raised the corner of her lips into a smile. My tears dripped from my eyes. Her once lively eyes had turned dull and lifeless. They were fixed on me. I could see the sadness in her soul. My quivering hand reached out for her but her head lowered. As she sighed, her hand rose, the tight grip on the object scared me and I darted out of the room. Eventually the corridors spiralled, like a never-ending labyrinth.

Hannah Archer (13)
Moseley Park School, Bilston

THE CLOWN OF MAPLE TOWN

Many things have happened in Maple Town, but the most spine-chilling was when 'it' struck. At about 9:30am, James was on his way to the shop when a clown teddy caught his eye. The doll was very peculiar and was always left on the stairs. At 7pm it began, James heard a voice, '1, 2, I'm coming for you. 3, 4, I'm opening the door. 5, 6, 7, 8 and 9, your mum's life is on the line. 10, 11, 12 and 13, your mum's life has been wiped clean.'
James was never seen again and the murders continued.

CHARLIE VINCENT (12)
Moseley Park School, Bilston

An Unknown World

He walked into the unknown. It was dark. Down the alley he smelt something sweet. He ran towards it. He saw what the sweet, soothing smell was - human flesh. Another ghoul was feeding on it. 'This is my turf, leave!' the ghoul screamed, but he couldn't. He pinned him against a wall. 'Please… let me go!' Kankei pleaded, trying to push him away. His grip got tighter. He broke free and ran. He was starving but he couldn't eat… but he needed it to survive! To survive an unknown world.

Lucie Beddow
Moseley Park School, Bilston

THE HOUSE OF HORROR

On a stormy night, Mark Wood entered the house of horrors on Churchill Street. He always tossed and turned on cold nights, he heard walls creak, floors squeak and the wind tormented him with its howling. He would hear dog attacks and gunshots close by. Mark would rock in the corner, pulling his hair out, wishing they would go away. Now he wished he had never left the house to investigate that night. Now he feared for his life as he hid under a lumpy, creaky bed in the Churchill Street house.
Bang!

MIA WARD (11)
Moseley Park School, Bilston

THE CHANGE

Alex arrived at the shop for a loaf of bread, they had sold out so he had to walk another mile to reach the next shop. He purchased the bread and left the shop. Happy he had bought the loaf for his mother, he turned for home but someone was following him. Alex increased his speed. All of a sudden, he became dizzy, he had to stop. He could see his home but his legs were like lead, he wasn't going anywhere! Whoever was following him was right behind him.
'Excuse me young man, you forgot your change!'

OWEN GREGORY (12)
Moseley Park School, Bilston

GHOST PARTY...

It's my birthday. I'm having a party at a theme park at night. The theme is extremely cool. It's vintage. It's amazing. We all go on the rides, they are much better at night because all the lights are on. The luscious smell of fluffy cotton candy around my nose.

It is coming to the end of the night. Most people have gone home. The theme park seems abandoned. *Swoosh!* Special people stood in front of me. Mum! Dad! No, this is impossible! They're dead... or supposed to be.

MIA BEVAN (12)
Moseley Park School, Bilston

THE BANDO

Driving on the highway, I was going to discover a property my auntie had told me about. I finally got there but I knew right away something wasn't right; the yard was taken care of despite it being an abandoned house. The lawn was neatly mown and the bushes were trimmed neatly, at least out front. The back yard looked overgrown.

All of a sudden, I heard a creak in the distance. I tiptoed as quiet as a mouse, hoping I wouldn't be heard. I opened a door slowly and a dead body lay at my feet.

SEAN MUNGURE (13)

Moseley Park School, Bilston

THE ABANDONED BUILDING

They were the cameraman, Franco, and the journalist, Victoria, on live television. They were about to enter an abandoned, desolate building to see whether they should bring the once rich building back to life. The building was once worth billions.

Creak! The door to the building opened. There was an eerie silence in the air. As they walked in darkness surrounded them. They carried on, they were about to go up the stairs. Then, *bang!* The floor collapsed.

DILLON NAYYER (13)
Moseley Park School, Bilston

THE MAN IN THE ALLEYWAY!

There he was, slowly walking down the dark alleyway. *Ping!* His phone went off. He got a text from someone he didn't know. He opened the message, all he saw was: 'Run!' He started to run as fast as he could. As the boy ran, he passed a dark figure and stopped. The figure turned to face him, he could just make out the face of a clown! The boy ran faster, but the dark figure followed him, jogging fast. The boy tripped.
'Argh!'

AMBER BOULTON (12)
Moseley Park School, Bilston

REALITY'S NIGHTMARE

There was a bang coming from downstairs so I went to investigate. I muttered, 'Is anyone there?' There was another bang, it was even louder. I could smell something unpleasant.

Someone murmured, 'Where are you?' That was when I saw someone I didn't know. That was also when I saw a knife. My heart began to race, my eyes were getting blurry. I hid in my room, locking the door. It made a thud. He was coming for me now. I closed my eyes...

ALEX M J JONES (12)
Moseley Park School, Bilston

WHO'S THERE?

Who's there? As Emma walked through the dark, mysterious graveyard, she anxiously scanned the area around her. Suddenly, she heard a giggle. 'Would you like to play?'
She slowly paced backwards. 'Ow!' Her head hit the ground. She carefully opened her eyes and saw a nauseous-looking clown smirking at her. She quickly jumped and ran...

TIA LOUISE FREEMAN (12)

Moseley Park School, Bilston

SILENCE IN THE MANSION

The mansion's rotting stairs groaned and grumbled as I cautiously crept up them. Spiders in surrounding cobwebs scuttled away as I inched into a nearby room. An icy breeze sent shivers down my spine. *Stomp! Stomp! Stomp!* Heavy footsteps on the stairs alarmed me. This ancient mansion had been abandoned, but was I alone? 'Hello?' I whispered. 'Hello... ' Panicking and perplexed, I leant back against the wooden door. My eyes widened; my heart beat faster; my mouth went dry. The door handle turned. Silence. I reached for the handle and found that the door was locked from the inside...

ZINAL PATEL (12)
Moseley Park School, Bilston

Anonymous

Rachelle was taking her usual selfie, she struck an attractive pose and snapped the photo. However, she noticed that a dark figure was lurking in her bedroom shadows! Traumatised, she instantly turned around. Nothing... Intrigued, she anxiously took another picture. Again 'it' was there. With her heart thudding, she decided to take another, this time revealing the figure perched on Rachelle's shoulder. Desperate to find out who this intruder was, Rachelle chose to start a video, hoping to see the figure move. What a tragic mistake she made! Simultaneously, she plummeted to the floor, dripping with blood.

Luis Chrimes (12)
Moseley Park School, Bilston

The Followers

A storm awaited. Gun-metal grey clouds crowded the sky, like an army ready to strike. Luckily, Amelia and Ollie discovered an isolated building to take cover in. Inside, only a tea light candle was visible. Unfortunately, the draught cruelly blew it out. Loud, heavy breathing could be heard. Startled, they spun around. Red orbs drifted about. Frightened, Amelia ran towards the door, Ollie followed. Before she reached it, it slammed shut. They ran around frantically, searching for additional escapes. Every door slammed shut. It became clear that whatever it was wanted what they had. Life.

Lauren Thomas (13)
Moseley Park School, Bilston

BLINK ONCE, NOT TWICE!

I was doing my job as a detective, investigating a disappearance at an abandoned building. The lift doors were stuck in the middle and the wooden stairs were on their last legs. Covered in cobwebs, the door creaked open. Piercing screams and whispers repeated what I'd read on a poster in the hallway. 'Whatever you see is in your head, blink twice and it shall disappear.' Terrified, I stumbled into the room the noise had originated from, moving the curtains aside on the rusty pole. I peered inside. A bright ray of light made me blink once then twice. Darkness.

PRIYA MADHAR (12)
Moseley Park School, Bilston

Keep The Lights Out

I regret it. I hate moving, it's always the same reason, to get away from my 'mental dad'. I always lose my friends. I hate it. However, this house sounds cool. It's silent and I can't sleep. Then I'm disturbed. I'm not alone. I hear singing. I slowly twist the handle and walk in. The singing stops. I stop. There isn't that much light, a cracked china doll is sitting there, it starts laughing. The light is wiped out. Something touches my shoulder. I feel heavy breathing on my neck, it whispers, 'Make sure you keep the lights out.'

Taliyah Sprackling (12)
Moseley Park School, Bilston

THE CALL

Emma Swan lay awake, scrolling through text messages, the light from her phone reflected on her face. The lamp on her bedside table was turned off so her phone was her only light source. The Star Wars theme tune blasted through the speaker. Someone was calling her. The contact name was unknown. Despite her worry, Emma answered the call. 'Get out!' warned a dark, gruff voice, one that Emma found unrecognisable. Emma's brows knitted together. She was about to ask what the person meant but they hung up. A loud bang from downstairs interrupted her thoughts...

FAITH WARRENDER (11)
Moseley Park School, Bilston

The Mirror

Naomi's eyelashes blinked gracefully. When her eyes opened she could see nothing except a mirror filled with dark substances. Her image was gone. The ghostly spirits slithered around her head, trying to possess her lonely mind. Naomi's arms shivered with dark thoughts. Naomi turned around and she saw a shadowy figure staring at her hazel eyes. The figure crept closer and closer towards her. Naomi felt like the walls were slowly consuming her. The figure backed Naomi slowly into a small corner. Naomi was extremely petrified. There was no escape for poor Naomi.

Symran Govindan (13)

Moseley Park School, Bilston

SIGNED... A!

As she wandered through the chilled corridors of an abandoned house, goosebumps shot up her arms. As she looked around she saw words written in blood-red paint, or so she thought. She crept around. She realised they were all signed: 'A'. She just ignored it and walked further into the house. She trembled in fear. Suddenly, she heard a noise, it was coming from inside the locked room. 'Come in and find me, I only want to play. I won't hurt you.' As the door handle slowly turned, cold hands suddenly crept around her thin waist. She shrieked...

ANNA LOCKLEY (13)

Moseley Park School, Bilston

THE GAMBLER

Annie came out of the casino with a distraught appearance as it was drizzling, thundering and lightning flashed to the ground. She looked at her watch, 12:00 on the dot. Once she'd sauntered off, a disfigured silhouette of a person burst out from the shadows, it followed her. Annie was in a suburban town under an echoing bridge. Annie always heard tiny footsteps behind her, although when she turned around no one was there. As always, Annie took a risk and shouted, 'Who is there?' No response. The lone crow screamed. Then something tapped her shoulder...

LEWIS CHAMBERLAIN (13)
Moseley Park School, Bilston

UNTITLED

One day, some kids decided to explore an abandoned old factory at midnight, close to a big city. When they went inside the massive factory the door opened automatically. They were scared but they still went inside. They went to the machine room and saw an inky dark shadow. They could hear footsteps getting closer and closer. The kids panicked so they all ran but it was too late because the factory was now a labyrinth. Eventually, the children got home. They didn't talk to anyone because they were terrified. The black shadow came for revenge every single night.

UDIET KUMAR (12)

Moseley Park School, Bilston

LEFT BEHIND

Visiting time was over, the visitor had been forgotten about and left behind. The prison had been disused for 60 years. It was located miles from civilisation. She saw derelict prison cells and broken glass. The woman could hear unknown footsteps. Suddenly, the isolated woman heard a petrifying scream from one of the now unused infirmaries. Her heart raced and beat like a drum. Rapidly, she sprinted through the maze of cell blocks. Then she stopped. A shadow stood behind her. The woman froze in fear. She looked backwards and was brutally slaughtered. Who was it?

VIVEK TOORA (12)

Moseley Park School, Bilston

THE CELLAR

Bang! The gigantic door slammed shut as I walked into the derelict mansion. I stumbled into this isolated building, I got incredibly lost and I needed help getting home. I shouted for help, no one answered. Quickly, I sped up the old stairs like a cheetah. I heard a young boy laughing. Slowly, a daunting doll started crawling towards me. My mouth opened and I screamed like a petrified girl, a spine-chilling hand dragged me down the stairs. Rapidly, my heart pounded and I was unexpectedly thrown into a cellar. I felt warm air. I heard heavy breathing...

ASHTON GHERA (12)
Moseley Park School, Bilston

GONE

Dark, damp, dying, were the only things Rebecca could think of. She looked around slowly, trying desperately to remember what had happened and where she was. Nothing, her mind was blank and her head was spinning, making her feel like she was going to be sick. She attempted to stand up but failed. She felt a searing pain in her stomach, she groaned loudly as her vision became blurry and then she realised she was chained to the wall. The only thing she could remember was being grabbed at the cemetery, she was visiting her mum. Then darkness...

MIA BHATTI (12)
Moseley Park School, Bilston

The Asylum

It was foggy and the rain was coming down heavily. James was a journalist, looking for an abandoned asylum in the middle of the woods. It was horrifying. After hours, he found it and pushed through the gates. He was instantly met with a horrid smell and an even worse sight - there were bodies everywhere! He went inside because he heard whispers. He went through the large metal doors and was instantly pounced on by three psychopaths! A huge mob charged towards him while he fought back. It didn't work! The last thing he saw was a hatchet.

Ellis Savory (12)
Moseley Park School, Bilston

PARANOIA

Walking home, I knew it was following me. I turned around and saw nothing but my own shadow. 'I'm so paranoid,' I joked to myself, strolling down the narrow street. As I approached the dark alley leading to my street, I heard it again. Again, all I saw was my shadow, behind me, this time cast by a flickering streetlight. I walked through the gates of my house. Everything stopped. The crisp breeze of the night vanished, the light of the moon drifted away. I heard it once more. I turned around. The blood drained from my face...

JESSICA BADIAL (11)
Moseley Park School, Bilston

POP GOES THE WEASEL...

The laughs awoke me from my peaceful slumber. They were coming from my china dolls. I did a head count. 14. Annabelle was missing. 'Round and round the mulberry bush... ' I gasped, only one thing sang that rhyme, I couldn't look. 'The monkey chased the weasel... ' I hid under my bed covers to avoid looking. The monkey thought it was all but great fun... I slid from under the covers and faced the window. The handle stopped turning. I let out a piercing scream as the last line was sung. 'Pop goes the weasel... '

MACKAYLAH SUTTON (12)

Moseley Park School, Bilston

THE RISE OF THE DEAD

Thirty hours had passed. Timmy was trembling with fear, sweat dripped down his face. He ran from the fierce Clown Town brothers. They chased him through the dense forest that night but then something happened. He couldn't explain it. *Bang! Bang! Bang!* The clown shot his gun and it went straight through Timmy's chest. He let out a yell of intense pain and tumbled to the hard ground. He couldn't believe it was happening. It was the revenge of the dead. The Clown brothers wouldn't stop until everyone was dead.

HARRY SMITH (12)
Moseley Park School, Bilston

The Exam

Tick-tock, tick-tock. I knew I was going to fail that exam. It was inevitable but that was the least of my worries. Colossal hailstones smacked the window. I only looked for a second! Why did I look? There he was with the dreaded knife, staring at me with his dark brown eyes. He tried to force his knife through the window, aiming at me! A flash of lightning came and he disappeared. 'It's the stress of the exam, it's just getting to me, it must be my imagination.' It had to be. But who screamed? Was it me?

Alex Warner (12)
Moseley Park School, Bilston

SMILING MAN

It was late, the moon cast dazzling lights across the thick fog. I was going home. Oh god no, I couldn't make it. I had to go through the field. Quickly turning my phone light on, I dashed into the damp, cold grass. I found a small derelict farm. The wind danced across the overgrown wildlife. Then I suddenly noticed a figure standing opposite me. I came closer. The man stood motionless with unblinking eyes, a smile smeared across his face. His smile felt disturbing. Petrified, I sprinted away. I felt a cold hand on my shoulder...

JAMIE BROMLEY (12)

Moseley Park School, Bilston

DON'T MOVE!

My tired eyes opened a little. I was on a cold, hard floor of
what looked like an abandoned house. Where was I? I felt a
cold hand on my shoulder. My head spun around but no one
was there. 'Don't move!' said a whispered voice. My whole
body froze. I moved my legs and stood up, something
pushed me back down. Another whisper said, 'Don't move
or you'll regret it!' I was hoping this was all a dream. I
noticed a doorway and a dark figure standing there, staring.
That was when I remembered what had happened...

EMILY BOYLE (12)
Moseley Park School, Bilston

I WANT YOUR KINDLES

I walked inside the house, no signs of anyone. Suddenly, a creeping sound came from the stairs. Frightened, a small hand stroked my back. I turned around. Nothing was in sight. Another stroke. I was shocked, yet again nothing was there. I walked towards the stairs. *Creak! Creak! Bang!* The chandelier fell down right beside me. I walked towards the master bedroom. Weird sounds travelled my way. I was scared. I tried to escape but a bar swung at me, knocking me to the floor. Dazed, I scrambled to my feet but it was no use.

AJAY SEMIC (13)
Moseley Park School, Bilston

Rain

The sun warmed my face as I strolled through the tranquil park. Rays glittered on the lake, a breeze rustled the leaves. Hearing a twig crack, I spun to see what had made the sound. Nobody. Ignoring it, I walked on. Tired, I sat against a tree. I jolted upright, realising that something wasn't right. I gazed disbelieving at the scalped face staring listlessly up at me. Bloody limbs surrounded me. Panic filled my head. A horrific shape blocked the sun. The rain threw sharp, icy daggers as I lay bleeding, limbless, dying.

ALANA SOPHIA DELGADO (13)
Moseley Park School, Bilston

THE HANGING HORROR

It was a dark and foggy night. Ben, Jamie, Joanne, Sandra and Lauren were all exploring an opaque forest. They saw an old, wooden cabin and decided to venture further. As they walked closer, they could see a light inside but nobody was there. They walked up to the door, it unlocked itself. At first they backed away from the cabin but then they decided to go inside. They walked inside, the fire was dying out but they couldn't see anyone home. Ben heard a scream and suddenly disappeared. They ran, Ben was hanging from a tree!

DYLAN THOMAS (13)
Moseley Park School, Bilston

BURIED ALIVE

I open my eyes to unbreakable darkness. My head hurts and my legs feel numb. Where am I? Who am I? All of my past memories seem to be a blur. Wait, I can hear the faint murmur of voices. 'We're gathered here today to say farewell to Byron Jenkins and commit him to the hands of God.' My heart stops. I'm Byron. My brain explodes with confusion and dread. I bang on the walls of the coffin. I can feel myself being lowered into the ground. I scream until my throat aches. I'm six feet under. I'm buried alive!

SEMHAR FESEHAYE (13)
Moseley Park School, Bilston

SCHIZOPHRENIA

My footsteps echoed as I crept through the dark corridors. I could only hear myself breathing sharply in ragged breaths. I peered around as memories flashed before my eyes. I shook them off and looked at the once white walls. They were now a shocking scarlet red. I shook in trepidation and looked down at my trembling hands. I slowly made my way towards a mirror hanging on the wall. My dark hair framed my pale face, making my eyes look darker than usual. I held my unnaturally thin, bloody-red hands to my face. What had I done?

HAYLEE GLOVER (13)
Moseley Park School, Bilston

THE ABANDONED HOSPITAL

It was a dare. My friends and I went to explore a scary, abandoned hospital. We were scared and frightened as we walked where people had died. Needles were everywhere as well as broken floorboards and smashed glass. I stepped over the needles that were as sharp as lion claws. I could feel the wind flowing past my nose. All of a sudden, I saw a black shadow with white eyes hover over the glass. All of a sudden, the shadow tapped me on the back. I shouted, 'We need to get out before something really bad happens to us!'

CALUM GILES (12)
Moseley Park School, Bilston

IT CAME FROM HELL

I can't sleep. It's three o'clock in the morning. I hear footsteps coming towards my room. I really wish I could fall asleep, but I can't. I check my phone again, it's four o'clock. I can see my door slowly opening. The thing that enters looks like it has come from Hell itself. It has long horns and black eyes with red skin. It seems to be coming towards me. It kills me! I wake up. The time is eight o'clock and it's summer. I'm really happy it was a dream, or was it? Maybe it wasn't...

DANIEL LEWIS (13)
Moseley Park School, Bilston

TALL TREES

The moon cast dancing shadows on the trees as we entered the forest. The dim torches created a little light as we walked further. The faint sound of screeching crows blended with the distant screams. My mind froze. The smell of pine soothed my entire body. My hair slapped me on the face as the wind whistled through the winding trees. I was alone. My friends had left me. The screams got louder and louder. I didn't know what to do. I saw a light and went towards it. The screams stopped and I saw my friends hanged. Dead.

COURTNEY MARIE YOUNG (13)

Moseley Park School, Bilston

THE EVIL SPIRIT

The wind blustered with more strength as we crossed the Sahara, this was a warning about the oncoming sandstorm. We kept walking until we saw an old house. The door was open and it shut behind us as we entered. It was very dark and quiet. We lit a candle and as we turned we saw, in front of us, the picture of the evil and powerful Jack the Magician. Unexpectedly, the window opened and the sand blasted inside. We heard someone's steps approaching, closer and closer still. Suddenly, I felt a soft touch on my shoulder...

TARNJEET SINGH (13)
Moseley Park School, Bilston

Stuck In Hell

It struck midnight. Kyle was still in school, the bell rang non-stop. He heard a loud squeal. He leapt out of his skin. All he could hear was the deafening sound of the bell. *Bang!* Out of the mist came a mysterious killer with a huge knife dripping with thick blood. Kyle froze instantly. Trapped, he thought that it was the end. Kyle started to run, the man chased him and Kyle slipped. Suddenly he looked up, there he was, staring at him in the eyes. The man wedged the knife into Kyle. 'Argh!' It was over.

Harvey Singh (12)
Moseley Park School, Bilston

Button Eyes

It was one of those days where I just wanted to endlessly stare out my window at the flashing lights and the cars passing. Lying in my bed, the feeling of uncertainty came over me. The lightning outside lit up my whole room. Unexpectedly, something strange happened. My red button-eyed teddy bear stared at me with a deadly, crooked stare. It vanished within minutes. I felt light breathing on my neck. I turned round. It tightly grabbed me. I gasped for air. My head spun in circles. It's still there waiting for me now.

Angelicca Louise Ludwig (12)
Moseley Park School, Bilston

THE MATCHES

It was a dark, gloomy, foggy day. The wind rushed past as he entered the old abandoned house. He was alone in the darkness. He reached out for the matches, the box was put into his hand. He quickly reached inside the box to get a match. He was too sweaty and weak to light the match. Trembling, he selected a match and slid it across the box. The match was lit and the room slowly lightened. There she was, staring at him, she said, 'What a surprise!' She continued, 'I didn't know you would be here... '

ADAM WATKINS (13)

Moseley Park School, Bilston

THE NIGHT CINDY WAS ALONE

Thuuud! went Cindy's heart as she walked up her creepy stairs. She could sense someone with her. Cindy was home alone! She climbed into bed. *Bang!* Her door slammed shut. She pushed this aside and tried to drift to sleep. All of a sudden, her steps started to creak like someone was walking up the stairs. She hid her head under the covers. Soon the door handle started to rattle. Cindy looked up. She was met by a masked man gripping a large knife. He bent over her bed. Cindy let out a scream...

ELLIE HAMMOND (13)
Moseley Park School, Bilston

THE GIRL IN THE BLACK DRESS

My mate dared me to make my way to an abandoned house, deep in the dark, mysterious woods. As I opened the door, I could see old paintings and I could smell lavender. A scream reached my ears as if they were laughing, a shadow loomed over me. A girl came, I started to sweat. My heart was beating like a bomb about to explode. She was dressed all in black, as if ready for a funeral. She grabbed my hands, I couldn't explain the feeling, I didn't know what to do. I went with the creepy girl, slowly, carefully...

VICTORIA MARTA BURY (12)
Moseley Park School, Bilston

HOUSE OF TERRORS

I approached the colossal doors of the mansion. I turned the old rusty handle and entered. Mountains of dust covered everything, I heard howls and screams. I turned to leave, but the dirty, damp doors slammed shut. I was trapped, scared and all alone. I crept around the house, hoping not to disturb anyone or anything in the house. The floorboards creaked as I snuck up the stairs. Lightning struck! I saw a shadowy form at the top of the stairs. I reached the top and heard something behind me. It was a dark figure...

MALACHI CLARKE (13)
Moseley Park School, Bilston

LATE SHIFT

I walk through the white, fluorescent lighting, it hurts. It's 1:45am, I'm counting down the minutes until I can go to bed but I have eight hours left of this exhausting shift. Not many patients other than drunks. We get the message that there's a mentally unstable man on his way to the hospital. This should be a challenge as most staff have gone home, leaving him tied to his bed, I rush to get a sedative. As I return, I can see him thrashing about. Are my eyes deceiving me? As I enter it stops...

KEON LIAM MAXWELL (13)

Moseley Park School, Bilston

THE PINK-CLOTHED PERSON

Another lonely day for Timmy working in the overcrowded theme park, earning nearly nothing. There was suddenly a scream that startled him. He did what he'd always wanted to do, become a detective! He snuck up to the woman covered in blood. He asked what happened. She told him that she was stabbed by a mysterious pink-clothed figure. The figure ran. Timmy panicked, he ran after it but a roller coaster derailed, almost crushing him like a bug. Timmy sprinted around it. The gun pointed at him. Was this the end?

ADRIAN FINDLAY OWENS (12)
Moseley Park School, Bilston

What Goes Around Comes Back Around

Thunder clapped its hands, rain poured rapidly. That was odd. When lightning struck I remembered what today was. It came to me like a flash. It was the day I'd murdered Simran ten years ago. I knew that her spirit would be coming for me. For revenge! I went to prepare myself for what was going to happen. I heard knocks on the oak door. I ran to my room. I thought I was safe until I heard, *bang, bang!* on the window. Simran entered the room, levitating towards me. I picked up what seemed like a bat...

Jaiya Bhathal (12)

Moseley Park School, Bilston

WHY?

My leg is trembling, there is an excruciating pain in my arms. What is happening? Why is it happening? Is someone doing this? My ankles are popping and before I know it my knees are bashing against each other. I find myself crashing to the ground. I use all my strength to get up but I'm completely paralysed. Immobile. My ears ring, my hearing grows weak. My eyesight goes. Darkness. But I'm still capable of hearing the intimidating laughter in the distance. It's taunting me, it did this. But why?

SIAN WHITTAKER (12)
Moseley Park School, Bilston

DEAD SILENCE

One dreadful night Nuke City had a vote to see who had to go to the abandoned fairground, Silent Hill Park. The city voted for me. I walked up the hill, full of anger because no one else was fearless enough to go. I started to look for the owner and Warren family because they were both missing. I walked through the park. The smell of toxic gas choked me. I saw gloomy skies. I felt the wet bushes. I heard the howling wind. One of the rides turned on automatically. I entered and the Warren family appeared...

RAFEEQ DE-BESSOU (12)

Moseley Park School, Bilston

THE HAUNTED FOREST

One stormy night, Kyle walked into the haunted forest. The forest was abandoned 750 years ago, it used to be a graveyard. The forest was cold and dark; there was no light coming from anywhere. As he walked, his goosebumps started to rise. He froze for a second, his heart was beating so fast he could feel it hitting his chest. Suddenly, a ghost appeared in front of him, he ran as fast as he could but he got lost and didn't know what to do. He never got out and he was never seen again.

KYLE SWARNN (12)
Moseley Park School, Bilston

MIRROR

Dun, dun, dun! I heard an alarming noise coming from upstairs. As I nervously trekked up the stairs I sensed fear. *Dun, dun, dun!* I heard the noise again. I gritted my teeth and surged forwards. I reached the bathroom and saw a freaky message that made my heart skip a beat. It was a blood-written message that said: 'Watch your back'. As I turned around, a knife slashed through my heart! I shrieked out in pain but nobody could hear me. I felt my body get lighter and lighter...

THEON MUKAMA (12)

Moseley Park School, Bilston

'TAG'

Looking up at the ghostly girl, she smiled and tilted her head. I froze, unsure of what to do. Should I run? Scream? No, what difference would it make? I had snuck into my school at 1am! The girl started laughing as she slowly faded away. She soon reappeared right behind me. 'Tag!' she whispered and as she touched me, my whole body felt numb, like she had just stolen my soul. I felt cold. Helpless. Alone. I felt like the walls were closing in on me and all I could do was stand there and wait.

FAITH ANDREWS (13)
Moseley Park School, Bilston

WE THOUGHT IT WAS ABANDONED

Jakub, Will, Najahe and I always went to abandoned places and today was no different. It was getting boring going to the same place every day. Then we remembered the abandoned serial killer's house. Some said he still lived there, others said he roamed the woods, looking for his next victim. We got closer and the smell of rotting flesh filled the air, that was when we saw it. The house was gloomy and foggy. We could hear someone or something, he came up to the window. He saw us and we scattered.

JAIDEN J HURLIN (14)

Moseley Park School, Bilston

ANNA

It was Sophie's fourth birthday, her mum and dad bought her a doll from an old lady's garage sale. She was trying to get money for an operation because she was blind. Sophie was so happy with her gift, she loved it! She was playing with it at night when her mum told her to go to bed. She fell asleep until she heard the crack of the doll's twisting head. She closed her eyes, not knowing what had made that noise. Then she felt something sitting on her. She fell off the bed and screamed...

SIMRAN GAKHAL (13)
Moseley Park School, Bilston

THE LIVING SPIRITS

One night, I heard the wind brushing against the window. There was a tree at the side of the wall and it looked like a wrinkly hand. The sharp branches were banging against the side of the wall. As I was going back to sleep, my door creaked and a light whisper said, 'You're next.' All of a sudden, a cold hand touched my leg. I ran out of the house quickly. In the distance I saw a light coming from an old abandoned cabin. It seemed like no one was home. I decided to go in, it was dark.

COURTNEY BARKER (13)

Moseley Park School, Bilston

THE SHADOW

Tony was a man who loved exploring, he was walking through a muddy forest as it rained. The trees were creaking, he ran to get away. His mom said that he needed to be careful but he never listened. He came across a haunted-looking house. He went closer to get a better view of it. He heard a girl scream. Terrified, Tony continued his quest. He walked in, the floor creaked as he tiptoed through. He heard someone say, 'Tony!' He looked. A door creaked open. He saw a shadow. What would he do?

JAMES ELWELL (12)
Moseley Park School, Bilston

THE MYSTERIOUS MONSTER

Once upon a time there were two young boys called James and Kyle. They were playing hide-and-seek in the forest with some friends. James and Kyle fell down a deep hole and it was dark. They saw something in front of them. It was huge, with glowing red eyes and fangs like razor-sharp knives. It was breathing heavily. The boys ran away and they came to the end of the dark, misty tunnel. They saw a mysterious old man. They saw that he had the same glowing red eyes as the thing that had chased them.

JARVIS HARTLAND (13)
Moseley Park School, Bilston

DOLL'S HOUSE

At last, I was in front of our town's popular toy superstore, I was so excited! It was my dream. Before I knew it, I had spent hours edging my way through every aisle. I glanced at the golden clock. 9pm? The store closed at 9:30pm, meaning I had 30 minutes. I realised that the only aisle I hadn't explored properly was the doll aisle. I closed my eyes for a second, taking a deep breath. I opened them and was horrified. Not only was I in the doll aisle, I was trapped in a doll's house!

LOUISE WALFORD (14)
Moseley Park School, Bilston

THE LAST NIGHT

'Help, help!' I yelled, I was trapped in the castle. It was pitch-black. I was freezing cold. I made up my mind to walk down the endless corridor. Suddenly, I noticed a shadow appearing in front of me. Shaking, rope was suddenly wrapped around my neck. What was I going to do? I didn't know what to do. How would I get out of this? I yelled and yelled, but nobody could hear me. 'Help! Help! Help!' I yelled at the top of my voice. I thought it might be my last night.

LOUISA CHILDS (12)
Moseley Park School, Bilston

THE LOG CABIN

As I walked on the dusty pathway, I could feel the rocks beneath my feet. The moonlight seeped through the trees. Walking a little further, I saw the rotten log cabin. The lights started flickering, I walked up to the door. I pushed and it creaked open. I slowly walked in, climbing over the old oak floor. I strolled up the stairs. A shadow lifted a table and threw it. The table hung on the wall beside me. The bang echoed around the room. I screamed, hoping someone would hear. It was too late.

TYLER FREEMAN (12)
Moseley Park School, Bilston

Negative Energy

My connection to the forest was always amazing, but when I went there one warm, lovely day it just felt cold, almost unwelcoming. The leaves were no longer light green and pulsing with bright positive energy, the crinkled, aged leaves resembled the touch of death; cold, dank and sombre. I felt like I had stepped into Hell. The sun beat down on me, pushing me downwards. The coldness chilled my blood. I needed to escape, as the thought compelled me to move, a gnarled hand grabbed my shoulder...

Tyler-Jade Linton-Phillips (13)

Moseley Park School, Bilston

HAUNTED HOUSE

One day, there was a boy and girl who ran away. At 12:00 they walked through the forest, they saw a big mansion. They said, 'Let's stay here for the night.' When they woke up they went to open the door. The door was locked. Then they heard a noise. They slowly went to see what it was. They saw an old scared man tied up. Then a man came behind them. He grabbed the girl so the boy hit the man and they both ran away. They hid in the cupboard until the police came to rescue them.

BRANDON LEE BAKER (13)
Moseley Park School, Bilston

The Haunted House

One day, my friends and I were walking down a dark alleyway. After a while, we stopped in front of a building. What was it? A dark, creepy house! My spine shivered when I heard the loud sound of voices and rustling leaves, we all walked up the dirty wooden stairs, the door opened like we were welcome there. We stepped inside and saw a large wooden staircase going up to the top floor. On the walls we saw old photographs of people who'd lived in the house. A cold hand touched me...

JESSICA THOMAS (12)

Moseley Park School, Bilston

PREDATOR

As I strolled down, the tall trees hung over me. The rain plunged down on me as I bowed my head. I leant up against the tree. I could feel the abstract patterns. *Crash! Bang!* A sound of thunder made me jump. A spark of lightning soared across the sky. I saw a mysterious figure ahead of me. Fog tiptoed in. I walked towards it. It stood still. I opened my wings and showed my fangs and it started to back away. I bellowed, 'I'm the only predator in the woods!'

DARNELL BODDIE (13)

Moseley Park School, Bilston

THE FRIGHT OF THE FAIRGROUND

My little brother, JJ, and I, Elveena Zenoby, were spending some quality time together. I told him to stay on a bench so I could get an ice cream for him. I came back and JJ had disappeared! I saw him walk into the abandoned fairground. I ran to stop him but it was too late. I continued to run through the rusty, rattling gates. I ran and ran but I couldn't see JJ. I heard screams in the distance. I finally found JJ, but it was too late. JJ was under a ride. *Bang!*

INDERPREET RAJASANSI (13)
Moseley Park School, Bilston

DEMON DOORBELL

On Friday 13th, Charley and Amber were having a chill night, just watching films and having take-out when the doorbell rang. At first they were debating about who would open the door, so they both went. As they approached the door the ringing got louder. They swung open the door to see who it was. There was no one at the door. They thought someone was playing a prank so they shut the door. They could hear laughing. Who could it be? He watched every step that they took...

CHARLEY MICHELLE LOVE (13)
Moseley Park School, Bilston

What Lurks In The Shadows?

He was alone in the dark. When he reached out for the matches, the matches were put into his hand. He shouted, 'Who's there?' He got no reply, so he lit a match and remembered that he had a lantern in his bag. He got it out and lit it. He saw nothing until *bang!* The door shut so he slowly walked up to the creaky door and slowly and carefully opened it. There was another door and two more either side of him. He walked closer. What was he going to do?

Georgina Williams (13)

Moseley Park School, Bilston

THE ABANDONED HOUSE

We skipped up the grassy hills, suddenly we were face-to-face with a gate. Behind the gate was an abandoned house. My friend and I opened the creaky door with cobwebs all over it. We went in. A doll and a creepy, pale girl stared at us. The girl locked us in a cupboard. I said, 'We're not going to harm you.' She let us out. She told us about her life. She was a ghost now. She said the house was unstable and we needed to get out quickly. *Bang!*

OLIVIA BADIAL (11)
Moseley Park School, Bilston

TEXAS MASSACRE

The violent night took the trees by surprise. Trees rocked from left to right like a cradle. It was a dark and misty night. There was a path and a forest. The boys were in a heartless, creepy, ghoulish forest. They were scared. Then a tall, black, dark figure took them by surprise. They noticed a sign saying: *There is no escape*. The figure looked like it was moving, it got closer and closer. In a heartbeat the figure lashed out, taking their lives away.

JAGVIR SINGH (12)
Moseley Park School, Bilston

THE ASYLUM

Thunder clattered as they slowly entered the asylum, as scared as ever. The asylum had been abandoned for 190 years now, people who entered it didn't disappear, they were only seen at night. They were reported to be some kind of ghosts. James, the youngest, was slightly shaking, but he still went in. As soon as they went in through the window, the whole world seemed to freeze. Terrified, Luke turned around, only to see that James and Lewis had disappeared.

CAROLINE BARNES (12)

Moseley Park School, Bilston

Dark Dreams

It was a stormy night. I was playing on my Xbox when there was a knock at the door. It was late at night so I didn't expect it. It was only my mom and I in the house so I just ignored it. I was about to go to sleep when the door sounded like it had come off its hinges. I went to look. I crept down the hallway and looked around the corner. I saw the rain pouring in. There was wood scattering across the floor. I had a feeling I wasn't alone. I screamed.

Vinnie-Lee Jordan (13)
Moseley Park School, Bilston

MIRROR, MIRROR

It was dark, I felt a shiver go down my spine. I wanted to go but the old Victorian door closed behind us. Nevaeh was fearless, she wanted to go into the basement. I clung onto Chloe, as she was the one with a torch. We wandered down a hallway until we got to a door. Nevaeh swung it open as if she lived there. I was pushed down first. I tiptoed down the swirly stairs. I heard a bottle smash. I ran back to the stairs. It wasn't a bottle, it was a mirror...

CHARLIE SMITH (12)
Moseley Park School, Bilston

Paranormal Activity

As I walked through the forest with my friends, we saw an old, abandoned house. We walked closer and closer to it. We got there and opened the door. We left it open. A ghost ran past and shut the door, making a loud *bang!* We were locked in. I planted my feet into the ground and a sea of dust smothered my face. I lifted my leg up to walk, but my feet were stuck to the ground. I was about to put my hand on the door handle. It started to shake...

Kiitan Adeyeni (13)
Moseley Park School, Bilston

THE CANAL PATH MURDERS

Mary could hear the sound of heavy footsteps as she hurried down the lonely canal path after dark. A man's hand roughly grabbed her sleeve and she spun around. Her legs were weak with fear. He was holding a gun and stared stupidly at Mary. As he walked towards Mary, she stepped backwards. Mary ran off and left the man. The man was waiting for her underneath the bridge. Whilst Mary walked she saw the man. She turned back around. The man followed Mary...

LILY KERRY BENION (13)
Moseley Park School, Bilston

THE BOY

The wind was howling as the boy rode home on his bike. The ground started to shake. It felt like waves. He fell off his bike, landing in front of a drain. He lay paralysed for a few moments until he noticed a bright red dot appearing from the back of the drain. He tried to get up, but it was impossible. With every second the dot came closer. He heard a hollow laugh as he came face-to-face with the person wearing the bright red dot. The boy was terrified...

SHANNON HADLINGTON (13)
Moseley Park School, Bilston

STORMY NIGHT

It was a dark and stormy night and Bob had to go to bed at 12 o'clock. He went to bed straight away. In his dream Bob thought his house was melting and that he had died. A few moments later he awoke, startled and confused. He went to get out of bed, but Bob slipped down the side of the bed and started to fall endlessly. There were screams and cries, but no one could hear Bob. He felt like he was falling forever into a never-ending abyss.

DYLAN CLARKE (13)
Moseley Park School, Bilston

THE SPOOKY WOODS

There was a family of four camping in the middle of the woods. It was dark and foggy and a lake was beside them. Trees bent over the tent. It was 10:30pm, they got ready to go to bed. *Crash!* An old, rusty tree fell onto the family's new white van. They dashed out of the tent. The van was ruined. Out of the corner of his eye, the father saw a black figure disappear behind a tree. He screamed. His son had gone.

RHYS DANKS (12)

Moseley Park School, Bilston

UNTITLED

One day, Thomas and his mother moved into a new house, a big house. Thomas unpacked his laptop and started to talk to the friends he'd had to leave behind in Madison. As the conversation went on he noticed a flicker. He took a closer look and out of nowhere a face popped out, scaring him. Petrified and scared, Thomas quickly turned off the laptop.

MUFARO CHUMA (12)
Moseley Park School, Bilston

CRACKS FOR THE SHADOW

They shut the door, trying to impede the perpetual flowing of chilly air through the cracks and crevices. It lurks and watches. Atmospheric shifts announce its presence in the darkness. Bodies tense and hearts flutter in the company of shadows. A foot dangles innocently from the bed, as if it's fish bait. Their pulses get faster, they breathe harder as they attempt to remain motionless, undetectable. Yet still the air becomes frozen, crisp as a December morn. Icy breath caresses their necks before swiftly being dragged out of the now broken window, into the night.

BOBBIJAY MCBRIDE (16)
Stoke Park School, Coventry

CAMPBELL CHURCH

There it is. Campbell Church. You walk through the crumbling gravestones and reach the rotten, tall gates. You hear the crows calling from the church spire and you push the gate, shivering. You walk up the cracked pathway to find yourself facing the door. Lightning rages to the ground as you stand and quiver with fear. The darkness grows darker with the first step you take inside. The dining room door creaks open and you want to take a look. You peer your head around the door. A cold breath creeps down your back. 'Finally!' whispers an excited, chaotic voice.

ADRIANNA DE-BLASIO (14)
Stoke Park School, Coventry

THE SHADOW

The crackling lightning tormented the abandoned house. It was dark and the rain was getting heavier, as it pounded against the windows. I sprinted into the house to keep dry. I opened the rotten wooden door. Inside, the wind howled as I ascended the wobbly stairs. All of a sudden, a spooky shadow drifted across the narrow hallway. 'Hello?' I called out. I got no reply. As I approached the white door, the shadow suddenly returned, this time it was gaining on me. I hurried to the white door and the mysterious shadow grabbed me…

ZULFAQAR ALI (14)
Stoke Park School, Coventry

THE WOODS

'If you go down to the woods today, you must not go alone,' was playing in the bushes behind the gate. As the leaves rustled and the tree branches made shadows of witches' fingers, there was an ear-piercing scream that broke the silence. Silence was restored as a stream of rich red blood and a shoe began to flow. I walked faster, lost; with no way out. I finally found an opening in the woods. *Bang!* Lightning came crashing down. Top halves of bodies covered the ground. I tried to back away. A hand stopped me...

YARNA PATEL (14)
Stoke Park School, Coventry

Lost

I didn't know where I was. I was lost. As I walked I could hear the crusty leaves underneath my heavy shoes. I was slowly marching to find a way out of the old forest, I could hear someone running towards me from behind. I turned around, nothing or no one was there. Rapidly, I started to run because I was terrified. On the floor there were footsteps like someone was there before me. It felt like someone pushed me from behind. I was on the floor, pulling my legs up. I could only remember yelling.

NATALIA BANAS (13)
Stoke Park School, Coventry

FOOTSTEPS

One cold and silent night, I walk on an empty street. Lights tower over the road, illuminating my path. Each breath I take becomes colder as the lights turn off. The street is in complete darkness. I can only see the dim city lights in the background, they give me a sense of direction. I hear footsteps close by between the trees across the road. I see nothing but feel a cold breeze flash past my pale face. As I reach for my torch in my pocket, I'm violently shoved to the ground...

AUGUSTINE UZOCHUCKWU (14)
Stoke Park School, Coventry

MY ETERNAL COFFIN

It all happened so quickly. I felt the boat below my feet jolt and collapse. Before I knew it, I was thrown head first into the icy black abyss I now inhabit. Every second I feel myself begin to shut down, each wave slices like a blade through my broken body. Struggling is pointless, it only makes the pain deeper. The water engulfs my mind and I lie still in my eternal coffin, a never-ending tomb of water. I allow myself to sink into it. I give in to it. I become one with the water.

SARAH ROBERTSON (17)
Stoke Park School, Coventry

Drag Me To Hell

The fog surrounded me, I felt a chill down my spine. When I passed the grieving gravestones, ravens screeched. I had nowhere to go. I saw the church and hurried towards it, my heart was racing. As I grabbed the door handle the door creaked open. The wind blew through the cracks in the wall. Tree branches bashed against the window. I slowly stepped forwards, my shivering hands touched the brittle bench. As I sat, something from underneath grabbed my legs and dragged me under.

Nafisa Patel (14)
Stoke Park School, Coventry

THE PIT

It was raining. The rain slapped my head, telling me to look for shelter. In the distance there was a manor towering above the skyline. I approached it, hoping that it would give me shelter. My hand grabbed the frozen doorknob and opened it. It creaked. *Bang!* I looked behind me in disbelief. The door had shut. Suddenly, a fuzzy sound approached me. I ran to find the sound, hoping it was a person. I felt air push against my feet. I had stopped. I was stuck in a hole.

CONNOR BELLAMY (14)

Stoke Park School, Coventry

UNTITLED

It's a place desolate in both space and time, forgotten by all. The sky, the earth and everything in-between work in perfect symbiosis to create a monochromatic abyss. This world of grey is disturbed by the bloodstained hands of one man. The sounds of frantic digging and the rustling of dead leaves break the eerie silence that encapsulate this forsaken land. He isn't the first or the last by any stretch of the imagination. His soul will forever haunt this land.

NIMO OMER
Stoke Park School, Coventry

A HAUNTING LULLABY

Slowly I step into the darkness. It's a place where no angels hark. It reveals a token of childhood. Steps quicken with a thud. I feed my intrigue as best as I can. A worn cradle and sullen table, an unused cot that time has forgotten. It lies rejected in the dark. Alone. A monitor hangs, suspended from the rafter. My ears ring with laughter, I see the toys start to turn, they cause my heart to throb. Now the darkness grows stronger and I realise I'm not alone.

TAYLOR STEVENS (17)
Stoke Park School, Coventry

FOOTPRINTS

Cold air filled my lungs as I hurriedly walked through the dark, foggy forest. Leaves crunched under my freezing feet. A loud, ear-splitting scream echoed through the forest, I ran. I didn't stop and I didn't look back. I came to a narrow footpath, there were huge footprints in the mud. Then, just when I thought I was safe, an old dangerous-looking man stared down at me. He laughed. I tried to run, but he grabbed my arm. I screamed for help but no one came.

MADDIE BROWN (14)
Stoke Park School, Coventry

NIGHT

My wet footsteps echo on a cobblestone street. Dim lights give solace on the enveloping night. I am late. My steps quicken as the night begins to giggle, the light begins to flicker. I am late. Running, I see faces on tall buildings. Running, I feel laughter's hot breath on my neck. I am late. A door, my home, my salvation. Shaking hands pull and slam the barrier between me and the laughter. The light is outside now, all I can see is blackness. I am late.

ALFIE TAYLOR (18)
Stoke Park School, Coventry

NO ONE HOME

There you are, driving down the abandoned road. Your car breaks down. You see an abandoned house. You go inside to get help but no one is home. You push the door with your hands and the door opens with a creak. You go in and you can only see a wardrobe down the corridor. You go towards the wardrobe and open it. There is nothing inside except a lever. You pull the lever and a hatch opens directly under you. You fall and fall...

MANVIR CHATHA (14)

Stoke Park School, Coventry

Est.1991

YOUNG WRITERS
INFORMATION

We hope you have enjoyed reading this book – and
that you will continue to in the coming years.

If you're a young writer who enjoys reading and creative writing, or the
parent of an enthusiastic poet or story writer, do visit our website
www.youngwriters.co.uk. Here you will find free
competitions, workshops and games, as well as
recommended reads, a poetry glossary and our blog.

If you would like to order further copies of this book, or any of our other
titles, then please give us a call or visit **www.youngwriters.co.uk.**

Young Writers
Remus House
Coltsfoot Drive
Peterborough
PE2 9BF
(01733) 890066 / 898110
info@youngwriters.co.uk